A Change of Plans

Megan looked up the number for Bachmann's and dialed. After three rings a man answered.

"I'm calling for Mrs. Alexander," Megan said. "We need to cancel our reservations for Thanksgiving dinner. That's right—eight adults and four children. No, we don't need to change them, just cancel them. It turns out we'll be having dinner at home after all."

The man was very polite and wished Megan a happy Thanksgiving. So why did the click of the receiver leave her with a sinking feeling, like she had jumped off a ledge and wasn't sure where she was going to land?

Smashed Potatoes

And Other Thanksgiving Disasters

Smashed Potatoes

And Other Thanksgiving Disasters

CAROL W. MURPHY

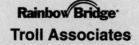

Rainbow Bridge
Troll Associates

To my wonderful family

CHAPTER
ONE

"Pass the ketchup," Jeremy demanded from behind the newspaper. He had propped the folded edge of the comics against the milk pitcher, making a little fort at the table, behind which, no doubt, he was talking with his mouth full.

Megan looked at Jeremy's outstretched hand and then at her parents. Her father's face was hidden behind the sports section, her mother's behind the home and garden pages.

Megan sneaked a pickle out of the jar on the table. "Here," she said, placing the dripping pickle in Jeremy's waiting hand.

"Yuck!" yelled Jeremy. He blindly flung the pickle away and it landed in the milk pitcher with a splash. He lowered the comics and glared at Megan. "What'd you do that for?"

"Oh, I'm sorry, Jeremy," Megan said sweetly. "I thought you said 'pickle.'"

"Will you children kindly settle down?" came a voice from behind the home and garden pages.

A firmer "Cut it out, *now!*" came from behind the sports section.

Jeremy grabbed the bottle of ketchup and disappeared back behind the comics. Megan fished the pickle out of the milk and returned to her sandwich.

Sunday lunch was always so boring. Megan took a big bite of her sandwich and made some choking sounds. Her mother peered around the side of her paper.

"Why don't you read the youth section, honey? Maybe there's something about your field hockey team in there."

Megan perked up at the thought of her name in print and leafed through the stack of papers until she came to the "Youth in the News" section. She read the headlines carefully, hoping to see MEGAN ALEXANDER POWERS IN WINNING GOAL. She turned each page slowly. Nothing. She started over, looking for at least some mention of her team. But the high school girls' field hockey team had won the state championships and that news hogged all the space. What a gyp!

It wasn't until her third time through the pages that Megan noticed the headline at the bottom of the second page:

STUDENT ESSAY CONTEST ANNOUNCED

She read on with sudden interest. "Hey, listen to this!"

> The Governor's Office is sponsoring an essay contest for children from 9-12 years of age. The topic of the essay is "What Thanksgiving Means to Me." The essay should be no more than 500 words in length. The winning essay will be printed in the "Youth in the News" section on December 1, and the contest winner will have lunch with the Governor.

At the mention of a contest, Jeremy had put down the comics and pulled his chair closer to the table. "I'm gonna enter that!" he announced. "And I'm gonna *win*, too!"

"No," Megan corrected him. "*I'm* going to win."

"You're too old," Jeremy shot back. "It says twelve years old and you're almost thirteen."

Mrs. Alexander took the paper from Megan and studied the article. "You're both eligible to enter if you want. Megan won't be thirteen until January, so she qualifies."

"I'll probably win though," Jeremy said. "I bet they give nine-year-olds special commiseration."

"You mean consideration," said Megan. "You can't even get the words right."

"Jeremy has a very good vocabulary," Mrs. Alexander said.

"See?" gloated Jeremy.

"And so does Megan." Mrs. Alexander ran her fingers through her hair. "Must you two fight over everything? Why don't you both do the dishes—you can fight over who washes and who dries."

Jeremy moaned, but Megan jumped up and worked in silence, thinking about her essay. When the last dish was put away she ran up to her room and sat at her desk with a clean piece of paper. Across the top she printed:

WHAT THANKSGIVING MEANS TO ME

Then she skipped two lines and wrote:

What Thanksgiving means to me is

She crossed this out and started over.

To me Thanksgiving means

Megan got out a new piece of paper, copied the title over, and then wrote:

Thanksgiving is a time for

She took a sharper pencil out of her drawer and copied the page over. She held the paper in front of her eyes and squinted until the words became a big blur. Suddenly she crumpled the paper into a little wad and tossed it into her wastebasket. Then she crumpled up the other page and threw that away. On a fresh piece of paper she wrote:

WHAT THANKSGIVING MEANS TO ME

and under that

(in 500 words or less)

Megan counted the words in her title. Five. This was harder than she thought. Still, five words was a beginning. Only 495 words to go.

CHAPTER
TWO

So, how's your essay coming?" Megan's mother asked at dinner that evening. "You certainly worked hard all afternoon."

"Great!" Megan said. "I got a lot done."

Actually, she still had 495 words to go, but she *had* organized her jewelry box and painted her toenails purple.

"I got a lot done, too," Jeremy said as he reached across the table for the basket of rolls.

"Don't reach, Jeremy," Mrs. Alexander said. "Just ask and we'll pass the rolls to you."

Megan gave Jeremy her best ha-ha-you-got-scolded face. Jeremy made a face right back and said, "Oh, right. The last time I asked Megan to pass the ketchup—"

Megan quickly interrupted. "How could you work on your essay this afternoon? You were over at Tommy's."

"But I was thinking."

"About what?" Megan challenged.

"Oh, just things. You'll see when you read my essay in the newspaper."

"Ha!" said Megan. "I'm really worried."

But she wasn't sure if she should be worried or not. It would be just like Jeremy to pretend to enter the contest, just to annoy her. Still, he did have a good vocabulary—for a nine-year-old anyway—and he did win that contest at school last year about the future of space travel. In fact, she wondered why he hadn't brought that subject up yet. He was always bragging about it and how he got to have his picture taken with the principal. Megan hated it when he bragged. She hated it even more when he didn't, like what he did was such a big deal that everybody would remember it anyway.

Mr. Alexander buttered a roll and looked at Megan. "So, what *does* Thanksgiving mean to you?"

Megan thought for a minute. "I guess what I like best is the food we eat every year. Mom always cooks the turkey, Aunt Edith always brings the pumpkin pie,

Grandma brings banana bread, Nana brings creamed onions—"

"Fish eyes, you mean," said Jeremy, "floating in that disgusting cream sauce."

Mrs. Alexander quieted Jeremy with a fierce look. "That's a good idea, Megan," she said. "What you need now is a theme—an idea that sort of holds everything together."

"Well, I like the way things are always the same."

"There you go," Mr. Alexander said. "That's your theme. Except you don't call it 'the same.' You call it 'tradition.' That means you do things the same way on purpose."

Jeremy poked at his dinner with his fork. "You mean like meatloaf three nights this week?"

"No." Mrs. Alexander said. "You call that a bargain. Food King had a half-price special on chop meat, so I really stocked up—you should see the freezer! But I'm sorry if—"

"It tastes delicious, dear." Mr. Alexander lifted his fork to his mouth, then paused. To Jeremy he said, "But if you keep making wisecracks, I'm sure we can make meatloaf a tradition. Hey, now there's an idea. I *like* meatloaf. We could have it *every* night. And why stop at dinner? We could have meatloaf sandwiches for lunch, and we could have meatloaf for breakfast instead of—"

"Never mind," Jeremy said. "Pass the ketchup." He

shook the bottle until his meatloaf had disappeared under a thick layer of red glop. "Anyway," he said, "it's not fair. You're helping Megan with her essay."

"The ideas are hers," Mrs. Alexander said. "We're just helping her organize them. We'll help you, too, if you want."

"I don't need any help," Jeremy scoffed. "I have my own idea. And it's original—not the same old stuff everybody says."

Megan tried to look bored, but she was secretly pleased. Tradition! That sounded pretty good.

Later, up in her room, Megan got out the paper she had started and read over what she had written so far.

WHAT THANKSGIVING MEANS TO ME
(in 500 words or less)

Under that she wrote:

What Thanksgiving means to me is tradition.

She counted the words in her new sentence. Seven. Added to the five words in her title, that made a total of twelve. On a scrap of paper she subtracted 12 from 500. Only 488 words to go. She'd be done in no time. And now she had a theme.

CHAPTER
THREE

Megan pedaled lazily down the road and turned into the driveway, coasting past her mother's car and into the garage. She tugged her backpack out of the straw basket on her handlebars and ran up the steps to the kitchen door. The smell of beef stew greeted her in the back hall. Megan hung up her coat and tossed her pack onto the closet shelf. "I'm home!" she called out.

There was no answer, but Megan could hear her mother's voice. She rounded the corner into the kitchen and almost tripped over a suitcase sitting on the floor. Her mother was talking on the telephone, the long cord stretched across the room to the kitchen table where she sat before a stack of notes and papers.

Mrs. Alexander smiled and gave Megan a little wave, then spoke again into the receiver. "That's right. Eight adults and four children. Yes, we'll need a high chair and a booster chair. Can we make the reservations for two o'clock? Good, that sounds fine. Thank you."

Mrs. Alexander crossed the kitchen to hang up the phone. "Hi, honey. Let me just write this down." She scribbled on the wall calendar, rubbing her ear with her free hand.

"What a day I've had," she said. "When I wasn't on the phone, I was cooking or doing laundry. So, quickly— how was school? Where's Jeremy? Do you want a snack?"

"School was fine, Jeremy stopped at Tommy's, and . . . what else? Oh, yes, I want a snack. But what's at two o'clock for eight adults and four children?"

Mrs. Alexander poured Megan a glass of milk and set the cookie jar on the table, talking as she worked.

"We've had a complete change of plans for Thanksgiving. Aunt Edith called me around noon, flat on her back in bed. It seems she was leaning over to change little Josh's diaper and her back went out. It was all she could do to get Josh off the changing table and phone a neighbor—you remember Mrs. Bell? Well, she's over at Edith's now, taking care of Josh and Andrew until I can get there. The doctor has ordered her—Aunt Edith, of course, not Mrs. Bell—to stay in bed for at least a week. So I'm going up to help Edith, and—"

"What about Uncle Joe?"

"Uncle Joe left yesterday for a business trip to Japan—isn't that the way things go? He won't be back until late next Wednesday, the day before Thanksgiving. Just how the doctor thinks Edith can lie in bed all day with two little boys to care for, I can't imagine!" Mrs Alexander muttered to herself as she circled the kitchen, wiping off the counters, stirring the stew, and doing a quick sweep with the broom. Megan had to pick up her feet as she sat at the table, her milk and cookies untouched.

Mrs. Alexander stuck the broom back in the closet and sat back down at the table, making a tidy stack of her papers. "So," she said, "I'm leaving this afternoon to stay with Edith and take care of Josh and Andy. And your father, heaven help us all, is going to run this house. You'll be in charge after school until your father gets home at five-thirty. I waited to leave so I could say good-bye to you all and give instructions on meals and things."

Megan took a sip of milk. "But you *still* haven't said what's at two o'clock for eight adults and four children!"

"That, my dear, is when the entire family is descending on Bachmann's for Thanksgiving dinner. Your grandmother offered to have us all at their apartment, but they don't have enough room. And my parents invited us to their house, which is big enough, but that would mean a longer drive for everyone. We're centrally located, so this is the most sensible thing to do."

Mrs. Alexander plucked a tissue from a box on the counter and dabbed at her eyes. "Imagine," she said, "Thanksgiving dinner in a restaurant after all these years of dinner at our house. But really, it's the most practical solution, and I'm sure we'll have a lovely meal."

Megan put her cookies back in the cookie jar. "Isn't Bachmann's a cafeteria? Why can't we go to the Inne like we did for my birthday last year? That's so much nicer."

"Sweetie, it would be too expensive—remember, there'll be twelve of us. Even Bachmann's will cost a lot."

The buzzer on the clothes dryer sounded from the basement. Mrs. Alexander picked up an empty laundry basket and headed for the cellar stairs. She paused in the doorway, the basket on her hip. "This won't be an easy time for any of us," she said, "but I know I can count on you." She turned and headed down the basement steps, her voice drifting up the stairs. "When something like this comes up, families just have to pitch in and make the best of it."

The back door slammed. Megan heard the thump of

Jeremy's shoes and books being dropped in the hall.

"Put your shoes in the closet and your books on the shelf," she called. "*I'm* in charge now."

"You're what?" Jeremy strolled into the kitchen and stuck his fist into the cookie jar.

"I said, put your things away. I'm in charge now."

Jeremy gave Megan a blank look and disappeared upstairs, leaving a trail of cookie crumbs behind him.

Megan slumped over the kitchen table. She was sure her mother could count on *her* to help. But she wasn't at all sure about Jeremy.

CHAPTER
FOUR

S o, I guess it's just the three of us for awhile," Mr. Alexander said at dinner. "I wonder how your mother is getting along." He glanced at his watch. "She's probably at Edith's by now."

It seemed to Megan that her mother had been gone for more like two days than just two hours. She picked up a piece of corn bread and tried to butter it, but it crumbled and fell apart.

"Sorry about the corn bread," her father said. "I thought I followed the directions on the package, but I must have done something wrong. It said to add a cup of water, but I wasn't sure what size cup to use."

Megan groaned. "Dad, that means a measuring cup, not just any old coffee mug. But it tastes great. Can I crumble it up in my stew?"

"Sure. I guess I really should learn to cook. But don't worry, kids, your mother left us a full freezer and plenty of instructions. At least we'll be hungry when we all go to Bachmann's for Thanksgiving. That reminds me— how are your essays coming?"

Megan washed down some cornbread with a swallow of milk. "I was thinking about mine in school today during math. You know how it said 'five hundred words or less'? I figured out that if I could make my essay five hundred words—I mean *exactly* five hundred—I might get extra credit."

"Well, that's a thought," Mr. Alexander said. "But I think five hundred is just a general idea. The rules ask for no more than five hundred words, so the winning essay could be one hundred words, or even just fifty."

Jeremy popped a piece of corn bread into his mouth and started talking, crumbs flying. "Yeah, you think they have somebody at the newspaper office just counting words? One, two, three . . ."

Megan hated the way her father and Jeremy seemed to be ganging up on her. She glared at her brother. "You're just jealous because I'm good at math."

But Jeremy was still chuckling over his joke. "Can't you just picture the guy—probably wearing a bow tie and a pocket protector—with this little adding machine and miles of paper tape all over the floor?"

"It's not only the number of words though," Megan said. "I'm writing about all the traditions. The turkey is always the same, and the—"

Jeremy said, "It's not the same turkey, you know. Mom cooks a different one each year."

"I know that, stupid. I mean it looks the same, and the platter's the same, and we always put the mashed potatoes here"—Megan pointed with her spoon—"and the gravy boat goes over there."

"The table is the same, too," Mr. Alexander said. "In fact, it's the same table I grew up with. Your grandparents gave it to us when they moved into their apartment. This nice big table is one of the reasons we always have Thanksgiving dinner here."

"Almost always," Jeremy chimed in.

Megan's stomach went thump at the thought of Bachmann's. "I think Thanksgiving dinner in a restaurant sounds terrible."

"It sounds great to me," said Jeremy. "Mom said we could have a choice of vegetables—no fish eyes for me—and ice cream for dessert."

"I like ice cream," Megan confessed, "but not at Thanksgiving. Besides, who carves the turkey? Who says the blessing?"

"I'm afraid the chef carves the turkey back in the kitchen," her father admitted. "But I can say the blessing if you like."

"*Not* in a restaurant." Megan felt her face get hot at the very idea of her father standing at the head of a strange table, his head bowed, while strangers at nearby tables all dropped their forks and stared.

"All right, then, I won't say the blessing."

"Promise?" begged Megan.

"Promise," her father said. "Unless, of course, your mother insists."

When Megan sat down to tackle her essay that evening, she started a new page. She wrote TRADITIONS across the top of the paper and made two long columns. One she labeled "Food." The other she labeled "Other." Under "Food" she wrote:

1. Turkey
2. Mashed potatoes
3. Banana bread
4. Pumpkin pie
5. Fish eyes

"Shoot," Megan said. She crossed out "fish eyes" and wrote "creamed onions." Jeremy was definitely a bad influence.

In the "Other" column she wrote:

6. Table
7. Platter
8. Blessing

She stopped writing. What if her mother did insist on the blessing? What if everybody stared? Even worse, what if everybody at the tables next to them bowed their heads? And the people next to *them* bowed theirs. Would the waiters and busboys stop in their tracks, their huge trays balanced on their shoulders, until her father finally said, "Amen"?

Jeremy poked his head in the doorway. "I'm working on my essay," he said. "How do you spell succotash?"

"Look in the dictionary," answered Megan. "Under *S*."

"Ha!" laughed Jeremy. "So you don't know how to spell it either."

"I do, too. I just think you should learn to look things up for yourself. Anyway, what does succotash have to do with your essay?"

"It's an old Indian dish," Jeremy said, "made with corn and lima beans."

"I know that," said Megan. "How many words do you have so far?"

"I'm not counting. Well, I guess I'll go see if Dad knows how to spell succotash."

Megan turned back to her paper and put a question

mark after "blessing." Then, turning to make sure
Jeremy was gone, she took her pencil and wrote in tiny
letters in the margin:

Sahkatash? Suckhatasch? Sockutache?

CHAPTER
FIVE

egan slid her lunch tray along the metal rails, watching her plastic plate get passed down the line of workers on the other side of the counter.

"Potatoes, dear? Applesauce?"

"Yes, please," answered Megan. She studied the view. Hair nets. Aprons. Big metal spoons and pans. Beyond that, giant pots soaking in tubs of soapy water.

Megan reached up and took her plate from the shelf. Then she moved on down the line, taking a little paper cup of tartar sauce and a dish of cherry cobbler. She stared at her lunch tray while the cashier made change.

Would her Thanksgiving dinner look like this, dished out in little plastic and paper containers? It would hardly taste the same as the food that came off the special china dishes from the corner cabinet at home.

Megan followed her best friend Amy out into the lunchroom and slid beside her onto one of the long cafeteria benches. "Just look at this lunch," she said glumly to Amy.

"What's the matter with it? It looks good!"

Amy always bought the school lunch, but not because she was too lazy to pack a sandwich at home. Amy actually *liked* the cafeteria food. She would probably like Thanksgiving dinner at Bachmann's, too.

Amy picked up a fish stick with her fingers and dipped it into her tartar sauce. "Don't you love these little cups they put the tartar sauce in? They remind me of candy cups for party favors. They are so cute!" Amy munched thoughtfully on her fish stick. "Hey, let's do our science project together. I liked the one you did last year where you grew the plants in water."

"What?" Megan answered dreamily. She had been counting the number of people at each of the long cafeteria tables. There were eight at her table, twelve at the next table over.

"What are you thinking about?" Amy asked, poking Megan's arm.

"Thanksgiving," said Megan. "My mother is away helping my Aunt Edith, so my whole family is going to

Bachmann's for Thanksgiving dinner. Bachmann's! Can you believe it?"

"That's not so bad." Amy dipped her half-eaten fish stick back into her tartar sauce.

"But can you picture my whole family—grandparents, aunt and uncle, cousins—at a table like this?"

"It won't be *just* like this. They have tablecloths, or paper place mats anyway. And chairs instead of benches. Hey, at least your whole family will be together. My sister and I are going to my dad's apartment. We'll probably have Chinese carryout in those little paper boxes."

"Chinese?"

"Yeah. It's like a tradition. We always spend Thanksgiving with my dad, and every year we eat carryout from a different restaurant. Last year we had Greek. The year before it was Mexican. Bachmann's doesn't sound so bad."

It was just like Amy to think everything was "cute" or, at the very worst, "not so bad."

Megan lowered her voice. "What if my father says a blessing?"

"Would he do that? Yuck!"

"You said it."

The girls ate in silence. Every once in a while Amy would try to say something nice, like "Bachmann's has great hot fudge sundaes," or "You probably won't even have to have turkey."

"But I like turkey."

Amy stopped trying to cheer Megan up.

Megan's whole afternoon was rotten until last period, home economics. Usually home ec was a waste of time for Megan since she liked to cook and already knew how to make cocoa and hot dogs. But today they had a substitute who let them cut out Thanksgiving recipes from old magazines. This gave Megan an idea.

When the dismissal bell rang at 2:50, Megan raced out the double doors of the middle school and into the school yard. She pulled her bike out of the rack and dumped her backpack in the basket. Then she waited.

Ten minutes later the bell sounded at the elementary school across the playground. Jeremy and his friends came bounding out the doors and down the sidewalk toward the crossing guard. Megan jumped on her bike and caught up to them.

"Don't forget," she called to Jeremy. "Mrs. Olsen will bring you home from Scouts."

Jeremy didn't even turn around, but his friends nudged him so she knew he must have heard her. Megan smiled to herself. There were a few fun things about having her mother away, and bossing Jeremy around was definitely one of them.

Megan sped ahead of the boys and pedaled to the corner. There she turned left and headed for town. This was not the way home, but with Jeremy at Scouts she could take her time. And she needed that time to think and to do some research.

CHAPTER
SIX

Megan pedaled along, full of a sense of adventure. She had never biked this way alone before. When she was with her friends, they were busy talking. When she was with her mother, the view flew by the car window. Now Megan looked around carefully.

For several blocks the sidewalk passed tidy little houses with painted fences and porch swings. The street widened gradually until it finally joined Main Street.

Megan paused at the corner. To the right were smaller stores—the Quick Mart, the shoe repair shop, the dry cleaners. To the left were the bigger, older buildings—the library, the courthouse, the bank, the movie theater. Megan turned to the left and felt her handlebars jiggle as the sidewalk changed from cement to brick and cobblestone.

After a few blocks the sidewalk turned back to cement again and the buildings became newer. Across the street, set back from the road, was a little shopping center with a hardware store, fabric and card shops, a pharmacy, and a supermarket. Megan had been to the Food King hundreds of times with her mother, but now it seemed different—bigger than she had remembered, with more people and cars.

She left her bike in a corner by the newspaper stand and struggled to pull a shopping cart free from the long stack in front of the store. The automatic door swung open with a *whoosh* as the cart passed over it. Once inside the store, Megan realized her cart had a stuck wheel. Should she go back and get another? She started to turn around but ran into other shoppers. This cart would have to do.

Megan headed for the first aisle, pushing her cart awkwardly. The stuck wheel made the handle vibrate, like her bicycle handlebars had on the cobblestone streets.

"Why, hello, Megan!"

Megan jumped to see Mr. Foster, her math teacher. "Hi," she answered, suddenly embarrassed. "I'm just doing some shopping."

She hurried ahead. What a stupid thing to say! Everyone here was "just doing some shopping," and there was nothing strange about being in the supermarket alone. Still, her knees were shaky. She felt like a spy behind enemy lines.

Her cart passed too close to a cereal display and knocked several boxes of corn flakes to the floor. Megan quickly shoved them back in the display and hurried on, hoping to get to the next aisle before the whole stack toppled to the ground.

In the dairy section around the corner an old man had parked his cart and was studying the labels on the yogurt containers. Megan parked her cart behind his and pretended to study labels, too. She picked up a package of margarine and looked at the tiny print, reading the details about cholesterol and calories until her nervousness passed.

Then she remembered her plan. She fished the magazine clippings from home ec out of her pocket, lined them up in the little basket at the front of the shopping cart, and started out again.

She went down each aisle, checking the prices of the items she would need and keeping a running total in her head. The jars of onions were $1.25 each, so three jars would be $3.75. Frozen pumpkin pies were $2.95—call it three dollars each—and she would need at least two. Added to the onions, that was $9.75. A ten-pound bag of potatoes was $3.19. Now the total was about thirteen dollars. Or was it fourteen? Had she counted only two jars of onions? Had she figured two pies or three? Either way, she was still on her budget.

She would need rolls or bread, and stuffing, but those would be pretty cheap. Was that everything? To be on the safe side she went down the last aisle. A banner hung over the meat counter:

ORDER YOUR FRESH TURKEY NOW!

Turkey! She had almost forgotten the turkey!

Megan read the details on the banner. Fresh turkeys ordered now would be ready to pick up next week. Didn't her mother always order a fresh turkey? As Megan tried to remember, a lady stepped up to the counter and pushed a red button, like a doorbell. The door behind the meat counter swung open and the butcher came out, wiping his hands on his apron.

"Yes?"

"I'd like to order a fresh turkey," the lady said. "About eighteen pounds."

The butcher took a clipboard from a nail on the wall and wrote down the lady's name and phone number. He didn't act mean, exactly, but he didn't smile either. He turned to replace the clipboard and Megan felt it was now or never.

"I'd like to order a fresh turkey, too, please." Her

voice sounded too loud, and she wondered if she was shouting.

"Name?" asked the butcher.

"Megan Alexander." Now her voice seemed too quiet.

"What?" The butcher seemed impatient, as if he might hurry off at any moment.

Megan repeated her name and breathed a sigh of relief when the man simply wrote it down.

"Phone number where you can be reached during the day?"

Megan gave her home number, then wondered if she should give the phone number of the school, too.

"Weight?"

"Weight?" Megan repeated, puzzled. "About ninety-five pounds."

"I mean the weight of the turkey," the butcher said. He didn't actually say "stupid," but his tone of voice did.

"It's for twelve people. See, my mother is away helping my Aunt Edith, so I'm—" Megan's voice faded. Clearly the butcher didn't care whether her mother was at the dentist or on the moon.

"Children or adults?"

"Both. Well, eight adults."

"I'd say sixteen to eighteen pounds should do it— twenty-two if you want leftovers for sandwiches and things."

"Twenty-two, I guess," Megan said. "My mother makes this great soup with—"

"Twenty-two it is then." The butcher scribbled on the clipboard and hung it back on the wall.

"How much will it cost?"

But Megan was too late. The butcher had already disappeared back behind the door.

She studied the price list on the banner: $.90 a pound. That would make it—good grief—$19.80! Megan tried to remember the old total. Was it thirteen dollars or fourteen? Adding the turkey would make the new total thirty-three or thirty-four dollars. This was just about all the money her mother had left in the jar on the kitchen windowsill at home, money for lunches and field trips and emergencies. Megan wondered if this could be called an emergency. She decided it could.

CHAPTER
SEVEN

The wall clock by the cash registers read 4:27. Megan's research had taken longer than she expected, but there was still time to beat Jeremy home.

Outside, she was relieved to return the wobbly shopping cart to the stack and find her bicycle where she had left it. There was a buzzing sound overhead as the fluorescent lights began to turn on in the parking lot. Darkness! She hadn't thought about that. A car drove by with its headlights on. This was going to be close.

Megan retraced her steps, biking back through town and past the school. Beyond the school the sidewalks disappeared, and the road gradually became narrower and unpaved. Farmhouses dotted the landscape, with lights beginning to appear in the windows and in the barns beyond them. The low sun vanished behind a cloud, and the air was suddenly colder. Megan longed for her mittens.

She counted the houses now—there was the Winfields', the Randalls', and Tommy's. At last, she coasted up her driveway. Megan quickly unlocked the back door and was still warming her hands over the kitchen radiator when Jeremy got home minutes later.

Jeremy disappeared into the den with a handful of cookies and turned on the TV. His jacket and books were piled on the hall floor, but Megan was too busy to argue.

First she wrote down the prices of all the groceries, adding an extra five dollars to the total, just to be on the safe side. Next she checked the jar on the windowsill. Forty-seven dollars. That should be enough. But if she had to, she could always borrow from her piggy bank. She took ten dollars out of the jar and put it in her backpack. Now it was time to work on her essay.

She was still writing at the kitchen table when the back door slammed and her father came in, juggling a gallon of milk and a bucket of chicken.

"Dinner," he said with a grin. "I forgot to take a meatloaf out of the freezer this morning. I guess we'll have meatloaf tomorrow night instead." He raised his voice over the sound of the television in the den. "Wash your hands, Jeremy. Time for dinner."

Jeremy bounded into the kitchen and plucked a drumstick from the bucket on the counter. "I'm starved."

"Put that back and wash your hands," Mr. Alexander said. "We'll eat in a minute."

"But I'm so hungry! I haven't eaten since lunch!"

Megan could see traces of cookie crumbs around Jeremy's mouth, but she decided not to say anything. She was feeling very pleased, both with herself and with her plan.

This afternoon she had finally solved the problem of her essay. There were eight categories—five "Food" and three "Other." Megan had decided to write fifty words on each category. That would be 400 words. Add an introduction and a conclusion at fifty words each, and she would have 500 words exactly.

Even better was the plan she had researched at the store. Instead of dinner at Bachmann's, her whole family would enjoy a traditional Thanksgiving meal at home, prepared by Megan herself. She would do the planning, the shopping, and the cooking, and surprise them all.

"What are you smiling about?" her father asked.

"Oh, things," Megan said. It had just occurred to her that instead of ice cream and a choice of vegetables, Jeremy would have to suffer through the traditional pumpkin pie and fish eyes. Perfect!

CHAPTER
EIGHT

The next day Megan remembered to wear her watch. She pushed up her jacket sleeve and checked the time—2:53. If everything went according to plan, she would be back at school by 3:45 in time to ride home with Jeremy after his band practice.

Megan hopped on her bike and rode quickly out of the school yard and past the yellow buses lined up in the street. She was out of breath when she reached Food King, but she had made good time. She parked her bike and got a shopping cart, checking to see that all the wheels worked. I'm getting good at this, she thought.

She pushed the cart into the store and headed for the bakery section. From her pocket she took out a shopping list and a ten-dollar bill. The list said:

> rolls (two dozen)
> stuffing

Megan had decided to start with the easy things. But as she searched the shelves she realized she wasn't sure exactly what she needed. There were more kinds of rolls than she had imagined. Poppy seed rolls, sesame seed rolls, potato rolls, sandwich rolls, sourdough, whole wheat. A bag of dinner rolls caught her eye. Surely that must be what she wanted. But there was only one bag like that. Farther down the shelf she found some party rolls in little foil containers. These would do, but they were so tiny that she decided she would need three dozen instead of two.

Megan put the rolls in her basket and checked her list. She walked down the long row. At the end of the shelves were boxes of bread crumbs, croutons, and— there it was—stuffing. Stuffing in boxes, stuffing in bags, stuffing for seafood, for pork, for chicken or turkey. Chicken or turkey—that must be the right kind. But did she need it seasoned or plain? Cubed or loose, in little crumbs?

She looked at her watch. It was 3:22, and she still had to go through the check-out counter! Megan read the labels. The small bag of stuffing was enough for a seven-pound bird. Suddenly she had an idea. She grabbed four bags: one seasoned, one plain, one cubed, one loose. No matter what, Megan said to herself, this has to be better than the stuffing at Bachmann's!

She rushed to the registers and picked the one with the shortest line. The lady ahead of her had two carts and had just finished unloading the first one. "You can use the express lane, Miss," she said to Megan. "It would be faster."

"Right, thanks." Megan pushed her cart down the rows until she got to the one marked EXPRESS. There were five people ahead of her, but everybody had just a few things. She pulled the ten-dollar bill from her pocket and smoothed out all the wrinkles. Out of the corner of her eye Megan could see the big wall clock. She decided not to look.

Her turn came at last, and the cashier ran the items over a scanner. With each *beep* the item and the amount appeared on a screen:

STUFFING $ .98
DOZ ROLLS $1.99
DOZ ROLLS $1.99
STUFFING $ .98

As the list grew, Megan watched with interest and then with alarm. She hadn't checked the prices! How could those little party rolls be so expensive? What if she didn't have enough money?

"That will be nine dollars and eighty-nine cents, hon," the cashier said.

Megan handed over the ten-dollar bill with a smile, but her hand was shaking.

"Out of ten," said the cashier. "Your change is eleven cents." A dime and a penny slid down a metal chute and into a cup.

Megan grabbed the bag of groceries and raced out the door, leaving her cart behind.

"Miss, oh, Miss," someone called. Megan jumped. Was she in trouble for leaving her cart in the store?

"Your change, hon," the cashier said, running up behind her and holding out the money. "Every penny counts, now doesn't it?"

"Oh, thanks," Megan said. "Thank you very much."

She didn't dare look at her watch until she had arrived, panting, back at school. There was a line of station wagons and vans parked at the side door, and Megan saw several bikes still in the rack. Relieved, she looked at her watch: 3:43. Only two minutes to spare!

"Your face is all red!" Jeremy said when he came outside. "And what's in your basket?"

Megan glanced down at the paper bag resting on her

backpack. "None of your business," she started to say, but decided that might just make Jeremy more curious. Instead she said, "Groceries, do you mind? Come on, we have to get home."

Jeremy raced ahead of Megan. Her legs were tired from her trip into town, and before long she could barely see his red jacket in the distance. Megan pedaled along slowly, thinking about her afternoon. On the bad side, she could see that she would have to plan more carefully—think about what she needed and what it would cost and how much time it would take. But on the good side, she did have a bag full of groceries, the respectable beginnings of a Thanksgiving dinner. And a twenty-two-pound turkey on order!

She felt sure now her plan would work, and today was only Wednesday—she had a whole week to finish the shopping and get things ready. Wouldn't her family be proud of her? And wouldn't Jeremy be jealous?

As Megan entered the kitchen it was obvious that Jeremy was already home. His books and jacket lay in a heap by the door, the lid was off the cookie jar, and the television was blaring in the den.

This gave Megan a chance to make a phone call, the last step in finalizing her plans. She looked up the number for Bachmann's and dialed. After three rings a man answered.

"I'm calling for Mrs. Alexander," Megan said. "We need to cancel our reservations for Thanksgiving dinner. That's right—eight adults and four children. No, we don't need to change them, just cancel them. It turns out we'll be having dinner at home after all."

The man was very polite and wished Megan a happy Thanksgiving. So why did the click of the receiver leave her with a sinking feeling, like she had jumped off a ledge and wasn't sure where she was going to land?

CHAPTER
NINE

Forty-two, forty-three, forty-four, forty-five," Megan counted. She read over her paragraph about banana bread. It was five words short of fifty, but she could add words to another paragraph if she needed to.

She set aside that page and got out another sheet of paper.

STUFFING

she wrote across the top. What should she say about

stuffing? Maybe the paragraph about stuffing should go with the one about the turkey. Megan underlined the word, then drew a circle around it. She made the *u* into a smiley face, and the *s* into a snake.

"Megan," her father called from downstairs. "Your mother's on the phone."

Megan raced down to the kitchen and took the receiver from her father. It was still warm.

"Hi, Mom," she said.

"Hi, sweetie. It's so good to hear your voice. I miss you all terribly."

"I miss you, too," Megan answered, suddenly feeling like she was going to cry. She did miss her mother, but she had been too busy the past few days to think about it much.

"I've never been away from you for this long before," her mother said. Her voice sounded funny, like she wanted to cry, too.

"Yes, you have," Megan corrected her. "Remember I was at camp for two weeks last summer?"

"But that's different, honey. *You* were away then, not *me*. I didn't miss you as much because I knew what a good time you were having."

"Aren't you having a good time, Mom?"

"Yes and no. I'm glad to be here helping my sister, but I worry that you all aren't eating right or wearing clean socks—you know, things like that. What did you have for dinner tonight? Are the dishes done?"

"Dad got us a good dinner, and the kitchen is all cleaned up."

"Who did the dishes?"

"I guess we all did." Megan looked over at the wastebasket piled high with empty McDonald's wrappers. "Actually, there weren't too many dishes."

Her mother said, "All day I've been thinking of things to tell you, and now I can't remember what I wanted to say. How are you? Is it boring after school now that field hockey season is over? What have you been up to?"

"Oh, not much," Megan answered, squirming a little. This wasn't exactly a lie, but it wasn't the truth either.

"What did you do today while Jeremy was at band?"

"I biked into town and went—um, I went to the library." Now this *was* a lie. Megan changed the subject. "How's Aunt Edith?"

"She's feeling much better, though today she walked around a bit and her back started to hurt again. The doctor said she needed at least a week of rest, and I'm afraid he was right. But Uncle Joe should be home in time for all of us to come down for Thanksgiving. Goodness—I almost forgot this is long distance, so we'd better get off. Can you put your brother on for a minute?"

When Jeremy came to the phone, he stood glaring

at Megan, waiting for her to leave the room.

"I'm going, I'm going," she said, but she didn't go far. What did Jeremy have to say that was so secret anyway? From around the corner she could only hear little bits of conversation. "Band practice . . . Scouts . . . substitute teacher . . ." Once she thought she heard her name, but she wasn't sure. Jeremy's voice was getting louder.

"How do you spell succotash?" he asked. "Dad doesn't know, and neither does Megan."

"I do, too!"

"Mom, Megan's listening."

It had been a trap!

Jeremy yelled around the corner, "Mom says you had your turn to talk and don't you have some homework to do?"

Megan felt hurt and ran upstairs. Jeremy talked quietly for a few minutes, then called after her.

"Mom says it's rude to listen in on other people's conversations. She says you're older and she expects you to act like it."

Suddenly Megan had a hunch. She tiptoed into her parents' bedroom and headed for the phone. Very quietly she lifted up the receiver. Just as she suspected—a dial tone!

Jeremy was still shouting from the kitchen. "Mom says you're not supposed to be bossing me around, that I'm old enough to take care of myself. She says—"

Megan ran downstairs and into the kitchen. "I just thought of something else I wanted to tell Mom," she said, grabbing for the receiver.

"Okay, yeah, bye!" Jeremy babbled into the phone and hung it up. "Sorry, too late!" he told Megan and strolled out of the room.

Mr. Alexander came into the kitchen and peered at Megan over his reading glasses. "What was that all about?"

"Just Jeremy being his usual bratty self, that's all."

Her father didn't ask for details. "It was good to hear from your mom, wasn't it? Sounds like she has her hands full. Today Andrew crayoned on the walls of his room, and Josh learned how to get out of his crib. Did Mom ask anything about, uh, my cooking?"

"Sort of. She wanted to know what we had for dinner and if the dishes were done."

"And? What did you tell her?"

"Dinner was good and we all cleaned up the kitchen—something like that. Was that okay?"

"Good girl. A few polite lies won't hurt."

"Polite lies?"

Her father rubbed his chin thoughtfully. "That's when you tell an untruth—a lie, actually—for a good reason."

Megan smiled. "Oh, right. Like when you're planning a surprise party and you say you were at the library but you were really at the store buying the . . . uh . . . the cake."

"Exactly," Mr. Alexander said. "A few polite lies may be necessary to keep your mother from worrying about us."

"You can count on me," Megan said. She felt better about the things she had told her mother on the phone. In fact, she was probably going to be telling quite a few polite lies before the next week was over.

CHAPTER
TEN

egan itched all over, but church wasn't the place to scratch. Maybe there was still soap in her clothes from yesterday, when she and her father had done the laundry. She looked across her father at Jeremy. Sure enough, he was scratching away, church or no church.

The congregation sat down, and Megan took advantage of the confusion to sneak in a few scratches herself. Reverend Thomas approached the pulpit and cleared his throat.

Megan always sat quietly through the sermon, not

listening but counting. Today she focused on the men in the front pews and had counted seven bald heads before Reverend Thomas's words caught her attention.

"And so, in the coming week," he said, "families will be gathering together to give thanks. And what will they be thankful for? Turkey with stuffing? Gravy? Cranberry jelly? Maybe three or four kinds of vegetables? Pumpkin pie with whipped cream?

"How far we have come from that first Thanksgiving, when people assembled in a clearing to give thanks for the loved ones gathered around them, for the food they had hunted or harvested, for the new home they had carved out of the wilderness. It was to give thanks for these simple blessings that the settlers . . ."

But Megan had stopped listening. Reverend Thomas had reminded her of two things she had left off her list. She took a card and a pencil off the little rack attached to the back of the pew in front of her.

The card said: "Welcome to our church. Please let us know if you would like . . ."

Megan flipped it over and wrote on the back:

cranberry jelly
whipped cream

"Nice sermon." Mr. Alexander shook Reverend Thomas's hand as they filed out of church.

"Yes," Megan added. "I really learned a lot."

58

"I liked the part about hunting and gathering the crops," Jeremy said. Megan wondered if she had missed something.

"Can we stop at the store on our way home?" she asked when they got into the car. "We need milk and bread."

"Sure," Mr. Alexander answered as he tried to tune in a good station on the car radio.

Megan ran into the store while her father and Jeremy listened to the news. She got bread, milk, whipped cream, and two cans of cranberry jelly and headed for the express lane.

"How are you today, hon?" the cashier said. Megan recognized the cashier from her other day of shopping but wasn't sure if the lady remembered her. The cashier's name—Evelyn—was stitched on the pocket of her uniform jacket. Megan liked Evelyn, who worked quickly but somehow never seemed to be in a hurry. She could make change and small talk at the same time.

"Let me guess," Evelyn said, running the whipped cream across the scanner. "This is for the frozen pumpkin pies you bought a few days ago, right?" So she *did* remember Megan after all.

Megan nodded yes, nervously watching her brother and father in the car outside, worried that they would come into the store and spoil her surprise.

Business was slow this morning, and Evelyn took her time bagging the groceries. "Aren't you a busy girl, in here after school every day! You've gotten the pies, and those little onions, and let me think what else—"

Megan looked out the window and gasped to see her father open his door and start around the car.

Evelyn was peering into the paper bag, arranging the cans and bottle of milk. "There," she said, placing the bread across the top. "We don't want *that* to get crushed, do we?"

"Great, thanks," said Megan, grabbing the bag and rushing for the door. But her father had only gotten out to remove a few leaves stuck around the windshield wipers. When Megan got into the car, he and Jeremy were so busy listening to the football scores that they hardly noticed her or the heavy bag. Megan remembered potatoes were the next thing on her list and regretted not buying them while she had the chance.

CHAPTER
ELEVEN

A my held a slice of pizza in one hand and took a bite, using her other hand to pinch the strings of cheese that stretched from her mouth to the slice. Megan decided to eat the pizza with a fork.

"I hardly see you these days," Amy said between mouthfuls. "Where've you been?"

Megan deliberately took a long drink of milk, thinking of what to say about her Thanksgiving plans. Amy would probably think her idea was "cute." But what if she wanted to help? Megan wanted to do this all by herself. Still, she felt guilty keeping a secret from her best friend.

"Promise you won't tell?"

"Cross my heart," Amy said, making a little *X* over her shirt pocket.

"Remember I told you my family was having Thanksgiving dinner at Bachmann's? Well, I thought about it and decided I could cook Thanksgiving dinner myself at our house—you know, surprise everybody. I've been busy shopping and—"

"*You're* going to cook a turkey?" Amy practically yelled out. "Do you even know how?"

"Sshhh. Keep your voice down. Sure I know how. I've helped my mother a zillion times. You just fill it with stuffing and stick it in the oven. There's even a little button that pops when the turkey's done." As Megan said this she got a sinking feeling. Would there be a button in the turkey she had ordered?

"What about all the other stuff?" Amy wanted to know.

"I've bought most of it, and I have a list of what I still need."

Amy laughed. "You and your lists! But I think it's a cute idea. I wish I could help you, but I talked my mother into fixing up my bedroom, and she's making me peel off the old wallpaper. You should see my room—it looks like the walls have dandruff."

Megan felt slightly miffed. Here she was worried

about how to keep Amy from helping, and Amy couldn't help her even if Megan asked. Well, that settled that.

"But, hey," Amy added. "I bet it will be a great surprise. I'll be thinking of you on Thanksgiving when I'm eating Chicken Mung Foo or something."

"Yeah," Megan said. "Wish me luck."

But she thought about all the groceries in the freezer and pantry and about her carefully planned list and felt she wasn't leaving much to chance.

Megan rushed out the school doors at the first bell and hopped on her bike. Today she would buy potatoes and be back in time to pick up Jeremy from band. She sang her favorite camp song to herself, changing the words:

> Monday, potatoes—Tuesday, turkey—
> Is everybody happy? Well, I should say.

Megan did feel happy. Excited, too, like when she had been in the school play last year and could hardly wait for opening night. The houses sped by, then the buildings. A school bus passed her as she pulled into the parking lot at Food King. She had made good time.

She was only buying one thing today, so she skipped a cart, went directly to the produce section, and pulled a ten-pound bag of potatoes off the stack.

Her knees buckled under the weight. She cradled the bag in her arms and headed for the checkout, hoping she wouldn't have to stand in line.

"Hi, hon," Evelyn said as Megan dumped the sack of potatoes on the conveyor belt. She dragged the bag over the scanner, "Now how's a cute thing like you going to carry a bag like this? Todd!" She called over to the next aisle. "Can you give this little lady a hand?"

"No, really," Megan protested. "I'm okay."

But Todd, a tall, thin boy, had sauntered over. He hoisted the sack onto his shoulder and headed out the door. When he got outside, he looked around. "Where to?" he asked.

"Just here," Megan said, trying not to look at her bike. "My mother's picking me up in a minute. Thanks."

Todd walked off, and Megan stood expectantly by the curb until he had disappeared back inside the store.

She picked up the heavy bag and carried it over to her bicycle. When she dumped it in her basket, the handlebars swung violently around and the bike toppled over. She tried again, this time bracing the bike against the wall with her hip. Again the bike spilled over, the potatoes landing on the ground with a thud.

"Can I help you?"

A lady was passing by with a little girl. The child stared at Megan with big eyes, one finger twirling a blond pigtail,

"Thanks," Megan said. "If you could just hold the bike for a minute, I think I can get it to balance."

The lady gripped the handlebars while Megan took out her backpack and set the bag of potatoes in the basket. She placed her backpack on top and patted everything down. "There," she said. "Thanks a lot."

"But can you carry all this? Do you have far to go?"

"Just a few blocks. Really."

The lady had that worried look Megan had seen on her own mother's face when she saw some child not dressed warmly, or out after dark.

"Poor child," her mother would say. "Where do you suppose the parents are?"

"Where is your mother?" the lady asked kindly. "Did she send you to the store alone?"

"Yes" Megan said. "I mean, no, she didn't ask me but I wanted to. It's a surprise." It bothered Megan that this lady might think her mother was mean, or not a good parent. She felt like she was going to cry. Sometimes it was easier when grown-ups acted mean instead of nice.

"Thanks for your help. I'll be fine, really." Megan walked her bike across the parking lot and out of the lady's sight. She wasn't sure if she could ride with all the extra weight, and she certainly didn't want an audience.

She continued to walk her bike through the brick and cobblestone part of town. As she turned the corner at Main Street, she heard the town hall clock chime in the distance. Megan took a deep breath and counted. One stroke: the quarter hour. Was it 3:15 or 3:45? She had lost all track of time and didn't dare let go of the handlebars to check her watch. The school was still several blocks away, and Jeremy might already be waiting.

Megan straddled her bike and put her foot on one of the pedals, pushing on the ground with her other foot to get up some speed. The bike wobbled along. The harder Megan pushed on the pedals, the more the bike jerked from side to side—now toward the street, now toward the houses and their picket fences. It took a wild swing over the curb and Megan jumped off. She would have to walk.

The houses passed one by one as she half-ran down the sidewalk. Her legs ached, and there was a pain in her side. She stopped to catch her breath.

In the distance she could see a steady stream of cars pulling out onto the road. Was band practice over? Would Jeremy know to wait for her?

Megan started walking again. She shifted her grip on the handlebars like she was holding a field hockey stick. She broke into a gentle run, chanting to herself.

"Alexander goes down the field. She breaks away— through the front line, through the defense. What stick handling! What stamina!"

She loped along in an easy rhythm, eyes half-closed as she listened to the imaginary cheers of the crowd. The school yard was just ahead now.

"Shoot!" roared the crowd. "Shoot! Shoot!"

As Megan reached the parking lot, the goalie stepped forward, leaving an opening. Megan took aim and shot. Score!

A pedal swung up and clipped the back of Megan's knee. The bike clattered to the ground, taking Megan with it.

CHAPTER

TWELVE

Megan dusted herself off and looked around. Only a few cars remained in the parking lot. The bicycle rack was empty.

The side door of the building clanged open and Mrs. Griffith rushed out. "Are you all right?"

"Where's my brother?"

"He was here a few minutes ago. I think he must have gone ahead. Are you sure you're not hurt? Do you want to come inside, maybe sit down for a minute?"

"No thanks. I'd better go home. Jeremy might be worried. He doesn't have a key."

When Mrs. Griffith had gone back into the building, Megan pulled her bike up and surveyed the damage. One of the leather straps on the basket had broken free from the handlebars. The basket hung awkwardly to one side, resting on the front tire.

Megan couldn't even walk the bike home like this. Maybe she could tie the basket back on. No, the leather strap was too short and wouldn't reach. Would Mrs. Griffith have a piece of rope? Or even some string?

"Boo!" Jeremy had sneaked up on her. "Where were you?"

"Sorry I was late. I had to do some shopping."

Jeremy looked at the bag on the ground. "Potatoes? You feeding an army or what?"

"They were on special," Megan answered vaguely. "And now my basket is broken."

"Well, I can't carry them," Jeremy said, nodding his head toward the trumpet case on the wire rack over his back tire.

"Maybe Mrs Griffith has some rope," Megan said and started for the building.

"Never mind that. I can fix this easy." Jeremy yanked a shoelace out of his sneaker, doubled it over, and threaded it through the basket and around the handlebars. He knotted it firmly and stepped back.

"There," he said with satisfaction. "Anything else?"

"Just hold the bike while I put this stuff back."

"You don't want to carry all that in your basket,"

Jeremy said. "Bad distribution of weight," He unraveled the string on the potatoes and reached into the sack. He stuffed a big potato in each of his jacket pockets and handed two more to Megan for her pockets. He took several more potatoes and put them in Megan's backpack.

"Wear this on your back," he said. "It's made for that anyway, and it's more efficient."

Megan was fascinated in spite of herself. "Where'd you learn all this?"

"Scouts, mostly. We're doing a unit on camping and backpacking. Wilderness survival—that kind of thing."

He placed the half-full bag of potatoes in the bottom of Megan's basket. The handlebars swung around, but the bike didn't fall over. "Now try riding—see if you're balanced."

Megan slid onto the seat of her bicycle. Her back felt rigid under the new weight, and her pockets bulged. She started slowly and rode in a big circle.

"Good! Keep going!" Jeremy shouted. "I'll follow you."

Megan straightened out her bike and headed for home. At first she had to concentrate just to keep her balance, but as she grew accustomed to the weight she had time to think. And there was plenty to think about. She played a game of "good news, bad news" with herself.

The good news was that she had gotten the potatoes.

The bad news was that she hadn't realized how difficult it would be to carry them home. The good news was that Jeremy was okay. The bad news was that she had been late to pick him up. The good news was that Jeremy had figured out a way to fix her basket and carry the potatoes home. This was also the bad news. The dinner was her idea and she wanted to do it by herself. She knew she should be grateful to Jeremy for getting her out of this mess, but she resented needing his help. He would probably brag to everybody about the part he had played in the meal—as if you couldn't have Thanksgiving dinner without potatoes. Still, he would be surprised along with everyone else, and that was worth something.

Jeremy followed Megan into the house, took the potatoes out of his pockets, and grabbed a handful of cookies. But instead of heading for the television in the den, he stood in the kitchen and watched Megan.

She emptied her pockets and backpack and put all the potatoes back in the sack. Then she carried it to the pantry.

"What?" Jeremy said. "No potatoes for dinner tonight after all my hard work?"

"No, not tonight. Maybe Dad will bring something home with him."

"Yeah, okay," Jeremy said. But still he just stood there.

Megan wondered what he was waiting for. She was

anxious to take inventory again and cross potatoes off her list. "Don't you want to watch television? Isn't that quiz show on?"

"I guess," said Jeremy, wandering off toward the den. In the doorway he paused. "You're welcome," he said.

"Oh, right," Megan answered. "Thanks. Thanks a lot."

CHAPTER

THIRTEEN

egan waited until the den door was closed and the TV was blasting before she went into the pantry. She took the list from under a bag of stuffing and made a check mark beside potatoes.

There was only one more thing on the list: turkey! Megan let out a groan and staggered back against the pantry shelves. Turkey—twenty-two pounds worth. Now how was she going to smuggle *that* home?

Her basket had broken under the strain of just ten pounds of potatoes! Today she had learned how to distribute weight, but she could hardly cut up the turkey and stick a drumstick in each pocket.

Megan started pacing the floor, thinking hard. How could she get the turkey home? She emptied her backpack and tried fitting the entire bag of potatoes in it. Not even close. A wagon maybe? Even if she didn't die of embarrassment, how would she explain pulling a wagon to school?

No matter what she thought of, she couldn't figure out how to get the turkey home by herself. And Thanksgiving just wouldn't be Thanksgiving without turkey.

How had she gotten herself into this mess? It had all started because she hated the idea of Bachmann's—the chef carving the turkey back in the kitchen, her father's head bowed as he said the blessing. That didn't seem so bad now. In fact, Bachmann's was beginning to sound pretty good.

If the whole family ate there after all, no one would have to know that she had tried another plan and failed. Well, no one except Amy, and she was sworn to secrecy. Even though Jeremy knew about the potatoes, he had no idea why they were so important.

What could she do with all the groceries she had already bought? Actually, they would keep until Christmas dinner, and Megan would explain them to her mother somehow—say they were on sale or something. Her mother loved a good bargain. And she could cancel the turkey she had ordered. Someone else would probably buy it.

Megan let out a long sigh. Now that she had decided the surprise dinner was off, she felt wonderful. She could stop playing mom and go back to being a kid. Maybe Amy would like help peeling off wallpaper.

All Megan had to do now was call Bachmann's and make the reservations again. She practiced some excuses, trying her most grown-up voice. "We've had a sudden change in plans," or "Something unexpected has come up." That was certainly true. Maybe they wouldn't even ask why she had changed her mind.

The kitchen had grown dark. Megan switched on the overhead light, checked the phone book, and dialed. The telephone rang several times before it was answered with a recorded message:

> Thank you for calling Bachmann's. We are closed on Mondays. If you are calling for this week's special menus, please stay on the line. If you are calling for information about our Thanksgiving buffet, we regret that our reservations have been filled. This week our special menus include . . .

Megan collapsed in a kitchen chair and just sat there, her mouth open, the phone dangling from her hand. A faraway voice droned on:

Friday is Italian night. Our menu includes
lasagna, veal parmigiana, and spaghetti with . . .

The den door opened and Jeremy burst into the
kitchen. "I'm starving. When's Dad—" He stopped and
stared at Megan. "Are you on the phone or not?"

"Not," Megan answered in a faint voice. "I think I'm
sick." Slowly she hung up the phone and headed for the
stairs. Her legs were so weak she could hardly climb the
steps. The upstairs hall was dark, her room completely
black. She inched her way along until her legs hit the
bed. Then she simply fell forward and buried her face
in the pillow, too unhappy even to cry.

CHAPTER

FOURTEEN

egan slept fitfully and woke with a start when Jeremy turned on the light.

"Dad's on the phone," he said. "He wants to talk to you. Are you still sick?"

Megan rubbed her eyes but couldn't make herself wake up. The light was behind Jeremy, casting his head in a shadow. His voice seemed to come out of nowhere.

"What time is it?" she asked.

"Six o'clock."

"At night? Is it still Monday?"

"Yes."

"Oh," Megan said, disappointed. She was hoping she had slept through Thanksgiving.

Jeremy scratched his head. The light was shining through his ears, making them look bigger. But for a moment Megan was reminded of her father and felt confused. It was as if she was the kid and Jeremy was taking care of her,

She sat up in bed and shivered. Then, wrapping a blanket around her shoulders, she padded down the hall to the phone in her parents' room.

"Hello, Dad?" she said.

"Are you all right, honey? Jeremy said you were sick."

"No, I'm okay now. I guess I was just tired."

"I have work to get done at the office. Can you stay awake and get Jeremy some dinner? I'll be home around nine o'clock, but you just call if you need me."

"Sure. We'll take care of everything." Megan hung up the phone.

"What did Dad want?" Jeremy asked.

Megan sat on the edge of her parents' bed and studied the wallpaper. "Have you ever noticed," she said to Jeremy, tracing the pattern with her finger, "that the flowers aren't lined up right at the seams? See how this leaf just stops right here, and then the end of it starts way up there?"

"What's the matter with you?" Jeremy asked, staring at her. "First you're riding all over town with potatoes that we're not eating, and then you're going to bed in the middle of the day. It's dark and I'm hungry, and all you can think about is wallpaper?"

Megan let her finger fall from the wallpaper and turned to Jeremy. "I've done something really stupid."

"So?" he said, blinking at her.

"I mean *really* stupid."

Jeremy looked interested. "Like what?"

"It's a long story. You don't want to hear it."

"Sure I do. Especially if you're going to get in trouble for it." Jeremy was not making this easy.

Megan started again. "Well," she said, "you know how we were going to have Thanksgiving dinner at Bachmann's?"

"What do you mean *were*?"

"I mean *were*. Will you just listen for a minute?"

"Okay."

"Remember I thought Bachmann's sounded terrible?"

"It sounded great to me—all that ice cream and stuff."

"And the blessing—that sounded great, too, I suppose, with everybody in the restaurant bowing their heads?"

"Who said everybody in the restaurant—"

"Never mind. Are you going to listen or not?"

"I will." And he did. He listened carefully while Megan told him about her plan, about all the food she

81

had bought and smuggled home. He didn't interrupt until she got to the part about the potatoes.

"I get it," he snickered. "I wondered why you suddenly had to have ten pounds of potatoes." Megan glared at him. "Sorry—go on."

"There's not much more to tell," said Megan. "Except—this is a bad part—tomorrow I'm supposed to pick up a turkey."

"A turkey! How much does it weigh?"

"More than the potatoes."

"How much more?"

"Twelve pounds."

"Twelve pounds total? Or twelve pounds more?"

Megan could hardly say it. "More," she whispered.

Jeremy pursed his lips in a long, low whistle. "That's bad all right, Why don't you forget the whole deal? We'll just eat at Bachmann's."

"Well, that's the bad part."

"I thought the turkey was the bad part."

"That was bad, but this is even worse. See, I cancelled the reservations Mom made. Today I called and tried to uncancel them. They're filled up."

Jeremy didn't say anything at all. He just sat there. The house was quiet except for the distant rumble of the furnace. The radiators clanked and hissed.

"So," Jeremy said at last, "what are you going to do?"

"I don't know. I guess I was hoping you might have an idea. You figured out how to fix my basket and carry the potatoes home. You're really smart."

"You're just saying that." Jeremy cocked his head and looked at Megan suspiciously.

"No," she said. "I mean it." And, for once, she did.

Megan eased several hot dogs into a pan of boiling water and began peeling carrots. She could hear Jeremy out in the garage, working on his idea.

"I'll think of something," was all he had said. When Megan crept over to the door and peeked out, he had shooed her away, saying, "Let me work, will you?"

She turned off the burner and tiptoed back over to the door. Through the glass she could see him bent over the workbench, cutting a piece of laundry line with a saw.

What was he going to do with a piece of rope? Was he planning to use it like a leash and walk the turkey home? Megan hoped he knew that the turkey was already dead and in no condition to walk anywhere.

"I think it'll work," was all he would say when he finally came in for dinner. "I'm starved."

"When will you know?"

Jeremy smothered a hot dog with mustard and relish. "Soon enough," he said.

Megan had to be satisfied with that.

She lay in bed for a long time that night, wide awake from her afternoon nap and nervous about tomorrow. What was Jeremy's plan? Would it work?

But no matter how stupid Jeremy's plan might be, Megan knew it was better than anything she had been able to think of.

CHAPTER

FIFTEEN

Megan looked out the window and across the school yard to the elementary school playground where recess was in progress. A girl was pumping hard on the swings, her hair trailing behind her as she kicked out her feet and leaned back. She climbed higher and higher with each kick until she was level with the top bar. The chain jerked, then caught again. Megan remembered her own days on that playground, the snap of the chain, that exciting moment when the swing just hung there, weightless.

Back then, she had looked over at the middle school and counted the days until she would be one of the big kids. Now she couldn't remember why she had been in such a hurry.

On the field behind the playground equipment, a group of boys was playing dodgeball. Megan recognized Jeremy's red jacket. Jeremy was "it," hurling the ball as if he hadn't a worry in the world. Maybe he hadn't. The turkey was really *her* problem. If they couldn't get it home, *she* would have to take the blame.

Jeremy had left for school early that morning, taking his secret with him. What was his plan? Would it work? Two more hours until school was over, and then she'd know. This was like waiting for Christmas. No, more like waiting for a dentist appointment.

The afternoon dragged until last period, home economics. Megan had her nose in a cookbook, studying table settings, when Amy grabbed her elbow.

"Look! It's snowing!"

Large lazy flakes drifted past the window. A few hit the glass and melted.

There was cheering in the classroom, and talk of a snow day tomorrow. Megan was probably the only one to think the snow was not good news. She had never ridden her bike in the snow before, and this was certainly not a good time to start.

By the time the dismissal bell rang, the ground was covered with a thin white blanket. Megan got her bike and trudged over to the elementary school, leaving big, soggy footprints.

The snow was wet and heavy. It stuck to her eyelashes and her bicycle tires. This was great snowball weather. Megan hoped Jeremy wouldn't abandon her to join in a snowball fight.

The bell rang at last. Jeremy came running out with his friends and picked up a handful of snow, packing it carefully. "Perfect," he said. He aimed it at the principal's back.

"Dare you!" yelled Tommy.

"Nah, I don't feel like it," Jeremy said and threw the snowball into a crowd of girls instead.

"You coming to Scouts?" Tommy asked him.

"No, not today. Tell Mrs. O'Neill that I had to help my sister."

"Oh, thanks," Megan said. "I forgot you'd have to miss Scouts."

"That's okay," said Jeremy. "This is more like Scouting anyway—fighting the elements and all that stuff." He tilted his head back and caught snowflakes on his tongue.

Megan was bursting. "So, what's your plan?"

"It's over here on my bike." Jeremy led the way to the bike rack. There was a familiar shape stuck in the wire carrier over his back tire. He dusted off the snow and uncovered his skateboard. "Pretty smart, huh?"

"I guess. But how's it going to work?"

Jeremy pulled the skateboard out of the carrier. "See, I've tied this rope to the front axle, so I can tow it behind my bike. I tried it this morning and it works fine."

"But can it hold twenty-two pounds?"

"It can hold me, can't it?" Jeremy coiled up the rope and stuck the skateboard back on his bike. "Come on," he said. "Let's get this over with."

The ride into town was slow. Snow kept falling in soggy flakes. The knobby tires of Jeremy's dirt bike cut through the slush on the sidewalks. Megan rode in his tracks, calling out directions.

His voice drifted back over his shoulder, "All right, all right. I know the way."

The parking lot at Food King was filled with cars.

"Just look," Jeremy said with disgust. "A little snow and everybody panics."

Inside the store, the aisles were crowded. Mothers pushed carts spilling over with children and groceries. Little old ladies and little old men carried baskets containing only a carton of milk or a loaf of bread.

Megan and Jeremy worked their way to the meat counter. Megan proudly pushed the call button—she bet Jeremy didn't know about that—and the butcher came out of the back room.

"Yes?" he asked wearily, looking around.

Megan stepped forward. "I'm here to pick up a turkey—the name is Alexander."

The butcher disappeared back through the door and returned pushing a little rack on wheels. The turkey sat on the top shelf, looking bigger than Megan had imagined. She gave a little shiver at the sight of the pale flesh through the heavy plastic bag.

The butcher came around the end of the counter and lifted the turkey into the shopping cart with a grunt.

"There you go, kids," he said, smiling at last. "Happy Thanksgiving."

"You, too," said Megan. "Happy Thanksgiving." She elbowed Jeremy, reminding him to say something polite. But he was just staring at the turkey, speechless.

Megan got nervous. "Doesn't it look good?" she said to Jeremy. "It's a fresh one, like Mom always gets. At least, I think this is the kind. Can't you just picture it all roasted and sitting on our big china platter? Well? Aren't you going to say something?"

Jeremy cleared his throat, "It sure looks bigger than twenty-two pounds," he said at last. "Do you think it's even bigger than my skateboard?"

"No," said Megan. "It'll fit. You'll see."

And it did fit, but just barely. They held their

breaths as they lifted the turkey out of the cart in front of the store and plunked it down on the skateboard. Jeremy tied the skateboard to the back of his bike and then pulled a second, shorter piece of rope out of his pocket.

Megan fidgeted as he began tying the turkey onto the skateboard, wrapping the rope around and around. "Can't you hurry?" she hissed. "People are staring!"

Jeremy tied the ends of the rope in a fancy knot and stood up, his face red from the effort. "That should hold it," he said, wiggling the board.

The turkey shifted a bit but stayed on.

"Let's get out of here," said Megan. She was afraid that nice lady from the other day—was it just yesterday?—would show up and start asking where their mother was.

"I'll follow you," she told Jeremy, "That way if the turkey falls off or anything . . ." Her voice faded away.

Jeremy started off, his bike wobbling from side to side as the tires skidded on the slippery walk. Behind him the skateboard lurched over the cobblestones. The rope would grow slack and then tug at his bike with a violent jerk.

Jeremy hopped off his bike. "It's no use even trying to ride," he said. "Between the cobblestones and the snow, I can't get any traction." He leaned forward, half-pushing, half-dragging his bike and its heavy cargo.

It was still snowing. Snow covered the roofs and little courtyards of the building. Traffic was heavy on the slushy roads. As cars slowly passed, Megan imagined people pointing out their car windows: "Look at those kids! Is that a turkey on a skateboard?"

Megan felt like she was in a parade, only backward. Usually the people stood on the sidewalks and watched the spectacle pass by in the streets. This time the spectacle was on the sidewalk. Well, she might as well make the best of it. She fixed her eyes on the turkey, naked except for the plastic bag, and held her head high.

CHAPTER

SIXTEEN

When they reached the corner of Main Street, Jeremy wiped his forehead with his sleeve and unzipped his jacket.

"You okay?" Megan asked. "Want me to pull for awhile?"

"No," he answered. "I'm going to try riding. It should be easier now that we're on regular sidewalks."

He climbed on his bike, made a few wobbling starts, and then rode ahead. But the skateboard wheels dragged rather than turned in the slush, and the rope jerked as the tiny wheels caught in the cracks.

After a few blocks, Jeremy got back off his bike.

"I'll have to walk," he said. "This would have worked," he added defensively, "except for the snow."

"Hey," Megan said. "I think you're doing great. Why don't I pull for awhile?"

Jeremy was happy to trade places. He pushed Megan's bike and she pulled his, surprised at the weight of the load. She stopped to unzip her jacket. She felt hot, but her shoes were soaked and her feet were freezing. She wished she had worn boots. The ground underfoot was wet like rain, cold like snow.

When they passed the school, they traded places again, walking side by side on the long, quiet road. The snowflakes were getting smaller. The wind had picked up and caught the flakes in little swirls. Megan felt like she was inside the little woodland scene in the glass dome on the living room mantel. She loved to shake the ball and watch the trees and fields disappear in a blizzard of white.

"It's pretty, isn't it?" she said to Jeremy.

Jeremy didn't answer. He plodded along beside her, his head thrust forward, his face set in concentration.

"I'll pull for awhile," Megan said, but Jeremy just shook his head and kept walking. He gave a little shudder.

"Are you cold?" she asked.

He shook his head again.

"Are you mad at me?"

"I'm just thinking," Jeremy said. "This is what my essay is about."

"What—how to carry a turkey on a skateboard?"

"No, I'm writing about the first Thanksgiving. Like how the Pilgrims had to face all those challenges— walking through the wilderness to get their food, darkness setting in, snow falling. Maybe wild animals— wolves and things—in the woods. You know, that kind of stuff."

"Sounds good," Megan said, though she wished he hadn't mentioned wolves.

Jeremy said, "See, if you look to the right, there are houses and barns and things—civilization. But if you look to the left, it's just forest, wilderness. And listen to how quiet it is. Maybe a wild animal is watching, about to charge at us from the woods."

Megan shivered. She was on Jeremy's left side, closer to the trees. "Let's change places," she said quickly. "It's my turn to pull."

She felt better once they had switched. They were passing Tommy's house. Lights glowed in the kitchen.

It was really getting dark now. Jeremy was becoming just an outline and a voice beside her. Their house, up ahead, was a colorless shadow. All that talk about wild animals had given Megan the creeps. She bent forward and quickened her pace, the bike sliding and hitting her legs as the skateboard tugged at the rope.

At last. The mailbox. The driveway. The garage. Home!

"I can't go another step" Megan said, trying to catch her breath.

"Well, you'd better! I bet that's Dad." Jeremy pointed to a pair of headlights slowly coming up the road.

He untied the turkey and grabbed one end of the bag. "Come on, I need some help. Where are we going to put this?"

Megan stooped over and took the other end of the turkey. "How about in the refrigerator? No, Dad'll see it. What about the back porch? It's cold enough outside, isn't it?"

"Good idea," Jeremy said. "Okay now, one, two, three—go!" They waddled awkwardly, hunched over, around the garage to the back porch. The wooden steps and floor were slippery under the snow. They set the turkey down with a thump and pushed it against the house.

Headlights played across the yard.

"Hurry!" Jeremy shouted, burying the turkey with handfuls of snow as Megan fumbled with her key at the porch door. They raced into the house and collapsed at the kitchen table just as the back door opened.

"I've been calling and calling," Mr. Alexander yelled from the back hall. "Where have you kids been?"

"Outside," Jeremy said simply. "We just got in."

"I thought so," Mr. Alexander appeared in the doorway, his shoes and coat dark with melted snow. "But I worried about you with your bikes."

96

"No problem," Jeremy said. "It was fun."

"Good," Mr. Alexander said, heading for the stairs. "Well, my feet are soaked through. I'm going to get changed. How about scrambled eggs for dinner?"

Megan listened to her father's footsteps overhead as she peeled off her wet socks. "Yuck," she said, looking at her wrinkled toes. "Prune feet." She leaned back in her chair and propped up her heels on the warm radiator.

"Hey, move over," Jeremy said and did the same.

Megan let out a big sigh. "I am *so* cold, and *so* tired, and this feels *so* good."

Jeremy reached across the table and held out his hand. "Give me five," he said, lowering his voice. "I can't believe we got that turkey home."

Megan gave his hand a slap. "Yeah, good work. Thanks."

Jeremy leaned back in his chair and closed his eyes. "Oh, shoot," he said, sitting up. "I forgot something I wanted to get at the store for Thanksgiving dinner."

"What?" said Megan. "Ice cream?"

"No, not ice cream. Succotash!"

CHAPTER

SEVENTEEN

Megan drained the hot potatoes and dumped them into the mixing bowl. Jeremy knelt on the counter, poised over the bowl, holding the electric mixer.

"Now?" he asked.

"Okay, now."

He pushed the dial. The mixer made a high-pitched *whirr* at first, then a low, chugging sound as it bogged down in the potatoes.

Megan took the saucepan off the burner and slowly poured warm milk into the bowl. "This keeps the mashed potatoes from being lumpy," she told Jeremy, repeating what her mother had taught her.

"But I like the lumps," he protested. "Otherwise, there's nothing to chew." He squinted at Megan. "Are you sure you know what you're doing? Mom never makes the potatoes the day before Thanksgiving."

"It's all right. I looked it up in the cookbook. You can reheat them. This way there won't be so many things to do tomorrow."

The beaters cut smoothly now through the mound of potatoes. Megan tossed in a big chunk of butter. It melted into a yellow swirl and disappeared.

"I think they're done," she said to Jeremy. "You can take the beaters out—no! Wait! Stop!"

She grabbed a dishcloth and wiped off the counter and the front of her shirt. "Next time," she glared at Jeremy, "turn the mixer off before you take the beaters out of the bowl. Just look at this mess."

"Well, ex-cuuuse me!" he snapped. "I don't know why I'm even helping. Here it is, the first snow day of the year, and I'm stuck inside like . . . like Cinderella."

"Sorry," Megan said. "You've been a big help. You can call Tommy back now if you want. There's not much more to do."

She scooped up a big glob of mashed potatoes with her finger and stuck it in her mouth. "Anyway, you're in luck," she said. "Lumps. Lots of 'em."

* * *

Megan sat at the kitchen table, puzzling over her essay. She had ten pieces of paper; eight of them were almost finished. The last two pages had only a heading at the top. One said "The Turkey," and the other said "The Blessing." These would have to wait until after Thanksgiving dinner tomorrow. Megan had started to write a paragraph about the turkey, but all she could picture was the big mound under the snow on the back porch. And when she tried to write about the blessing, she couldn't remember all the things her father always said. Tomorrow she would listen more carefully.

She was counting words—"three hundred and twenty-five, three hundred and twenty-six"—when the telephone rang.

"Hi, honey. It's Mom. I thought you'd be out playing in the snow!"

"Jeremy is." From the kitchen window she could see Jeremy and Tommy in the backyard, building a fort with the last of the snow. Tommy balanced the wheelbarrow while Jeremy shoveled on wet slush from around the yard. The fort walls were waist-high and dotted with leaves and grass.

"Mom, when are you coming home?"

"Your Uncle Joe is due in late tonight and we'll all drive down tomorrow. The major roads have been plowed, and what hasn't been plowed is melting anyway. We'll all meet at our house around one o'clock and go to the restaurant from there. Your grandparents are coming, too. They said they wouldn't miss it for anything."

"So that makes twelve, right?" Megan stretched the phone cord across the kitchen and opened the doors into the dining room. She smiled with satisfaction at the sight of the big table set with china and glass, and the eleven chairs and one high chair spaced evenly around the edges. There were still a few matted places in the rug where Jeremy had missed with the vacuum, but he had done a pretty good job. She closed the doors again. For dinner tonight they would have pizza in the den while her father watched the football game previews.

"What a morning I've had," her mother said. "The boys are napping right now, but I'm the one who's really tired. I've been pulling them around the yard in their little sled. No wonder Edith's back acted up. I had forgotten how much work two little children—"

Still smiling, Megan wandered across the kitchen and slowly lifted the cover off the casserole dish. Her smile disappeared. The creamed onions did look like fish eyes now, pale round blobs covered with a thick sauce. Some of the lumps were onions, some were flour. Well, maybe Jeremy would like these better. There would certainly be more to chew.

"I can't wait to see you all," her mother was saying. "Have you been eating enough? I bet you're tired of meatloaf."

"No, not really."

"I'm going to run to the market while the boys are napping. I thought I'd get some cheese and crackers for tomorrow, so we'll have something to munch on before we go to Bachmann's. Do you need anything? Bread? Milk?"

"Well, I was wondering. Could you bring some corn and some lima beans?"

"Succotash? First Jeremy, and now you. What's with the succotash?"

"Jeremy was just working on his essay and he wanted to try it. So, could you?"

"Sure. How's your essay coming?"

"Fine. I'm working on it right now."

"Well, you've been a big help this week. I knew I could count on you. Has Jeremy been giving you a bad time?"

"Not so bad. He's been helping."

"That's wonderful. I never thought I'd hear that. Maybe this will all turn out for the best. Remember how disappointed I was at the idea of Thanksgiving dinner in a restaurant? Now I'm really looking forward to it. After the busy week I've had, it sounds wonderful to sit back and let someone else do the cooking."

Megan peeked at the creamed onions again. "Yeah," she sighed. "That *does* sound good."

CHAPTER

EIGHTEEN

Megan sat up in bed and looked at the clock, worried that she had overslept. But only soft, gray light filtered through her curtains, and the clock said not quite seven. She dressed in the warmth of her bed and tiptoed downstairs. The quiet house felt like Christmas morning.

Megan flicked on the kitchen light and sat at the table, studying the recipe for roast turkey in her mother's favorite cookbook. She talked to herself as she scribbled little numbers at the bottom of the page.

"Lets see, cook for fifteen minutes per pound. Fifteen goes into one hour four times—that's four pounds for every hour. Four goes into twenty-two pounds five and a half times, so that means five and a half hours.

"Now, subtract five and a half hours from two o'clock. The turkey has to go in the oven at eight-thirty. I've got plenty of time."

Next she got the packages of stuffing from the pantry and read the directions, heating water and butter in a big pot and adding the contents of the four different bags. The dried bread rattled into the pan and then gradually softened as it soaked up the water. Megan stirred it all together with a wooden spoon, holding her face over the steaming mixture. It smelled wonderful!

Once again, she checked over the list, moving from the refrigerator to the pantry and back again. Rolls. Pumpkin pies. Whipped cream. Mashed potatoes. Creamed onions. Cranberry jelly.

Then she made a final inspection of the dining room. The rising sun poured in the window, bathing the table in light. The glasses sparkled, casting dots of color onto the walls and ceiling.

Megan felt a shiver of excitement. After all her planning, after all her trouble and worry, Thanksgiving was finally here. In a few hours she would surprise her entire family with a meal she had prepared all by herself. Well, almost by herself.

At last, it was time to get the turkey.

She took a few careful steps onto the porch, bent down, and reached for the snowy mound. But most of the snow was gone. And where the turkey had been, now there was nothing at all.

Very funny. This was just like Jeremy. She could imagine him—and Tommy, too, probably—dragging the huge bird off the porch and hiding it. Megan ran down the steps and across the lawn to the fort. One of the walls had melted and caved in. She dug her hands into the pile of snow, but there was nothing underneath.

She raced back to the house and up to Jeremy's room.

"All right," she said, shaking him awake. "Where's the turkey?"

"What?" Jeremy blinked and pulled the covers over his head.

"I said where's the turkey?" Megan yanked the covers back. "It's gone and I know who took it." She was shouting now.

Jeremy bolted out of bed. "I don't know!" he yelled back. "The last I saw it, it was on the porch—right where we left it. Honest!"

He looked so innocent, his hair sticking up all over the place, his eyes wide. Megan shuddered to think he might be telling the truth.

Jeremy brushed past her. Megan followed as he ran downstairs and out onto the porch, still in his bare feet.

He looked at the empty spot.

"It's gone, all right, but I didn't take it." He squatted down and peered closely at the little drift of snow. "Footprints!" he exclaimed.

"Those are mine," Megan snapped. "I was just out here, looking—"

"No, these." Jeremy pointed to some little dots in the slush. "Hey, neat!" he said. "Raccoons, or maybe foxes! We're studying tracking in Scouts—you know, animal prints, pathfinding, that kind of stuff. Let me get my book."

"Forget your book," Megan screamed, "and just find the turkey!"

Jeremy bent over, following the tracks across the porch floor. "See, there's a little path in the snow, like something was dragged, and more prints."

Jeremy wandered down the porch steps and started across the yard, his bare feet leaving a new set of prints. Every few steps he would pick up something and hand it silently to Megan—a scrap of plastic, a piece of torn label.

The tracks continued down the gentle slope at the back of the yard and disappeared into a thicket overrun with wild raspberries. There was a little opening at the base of the thicket. Jeremy dropped to his knees and tried to squeeze though. The prickly branches tugged at his pajamas.

"Ouch!" he said. "It's no use. But something's in there,

and it's got our turkey. Just think! I've spent hours trying to track an animal in the woods, and all the time there was something right here in our yard!"

Megan knelt down next to Jeremy and looked closely into the dense brush. The sun was quite high now, and she could feel the warmth on her back. Still, she started to shake all over. Her teeth chattered. She heard a little stirring and imagined two beady eyes looking back at her. Or maybe more than two—maybe a whole den of animals . . .

A tall shadow rose up from behind them and swept across the thicket. Megan screamed, afraid to turn around.

"What are you kids doing?"

Megan whirled around to see her father's angry face. He was in his bathrobe, his rubber boots unlaced.

"Jeremy, you haven't got any shoes on! Get inside, *now*. You, too, Megan. Don't you have any sense?"

Jeremy jumped up and looked with surprise at his blue-white feet. "You'll never guess what happened!" he said.

"Later," growled his father.

Megan and Jeremy started up to the house. Mr. Alexander followed, barking questions at them. "What have you been up to? What do you think you're doing, half-dressed, playing in the snow? And what's all the mess in the kitchen? The one morning I think I can sleep late, I find you outside, doing your best to catch cold. What would your mother say?"

At the mention of her mother, Megan stiffened. What was her mother going to say? Not about the outside-in-the-snow-part, but about the no-turkey, no-dinner part?

Jeremy reached the kitchen first. He wrapped his feet in a dish towel and sat down by the radiator. Megan was too nervous to sit. She just stood there while her father thumped the snow off his boots at the back door.

Megan's teeth were still chattering, but not from the cold. What would she tell her father? How could she even face him? This was scarier than raccoons and foxes. Scarier even than wolves.

Megan couldn't help it. Leaving Jeremy alone to tell the awful story, she turned and ran. And she didn't stop until she had locked herself in her room.

NINETEEN

egan lay in bed, staring at the ceiling. She pulled her pillow over her head, trying to drown out the sounds drifting up from the kitchen below. First her father's deep, angry voice, raised in a question. Then Jeremy's high-pitched voice, squeaking out an answer. Low voice, high voice, low voice, high voice. Gradually the sounds died down. Megan yanked the pillow away and strained to hear.

The bathroom door closed down the hall and the shower started running. There were heavy footsteps on the stairs. Megan heard rustling outside her room and a gentle knock at the door.

"It's me," her father said. "Can I come in?"

"Leave me alone!"

"It's okay, honey. We'll think of something."

Her father's voice sounded amused. Megan pulled the pillow over her head again and burst into tears. Amused was worse than angry.

"Go away," she sobbed into the pillowcase.

"Why don't you come downstairs in a little while? It'll be all right. You'll see."

The footsteps faded away. The house was quiet.

Megan took the pillow off her face and stared up, trying to memorize the star chart her father had taped to the ceiling before her science test last year. She pretended she was floating through space, surrounded by darkness, the earth a thousand miles away. Out in space there were no wild animals, no turkey dinners. No Thanksgiving. Nothing but space and silence. She closed her eyes and breathed deeply.

It was no use. The clatter of pans in the kitchen brought her abruptly back to earth. There was the muffled sound of laughter. The whir of the mixer. The slam of the back door. The high whine of her father's power saw.

Power saw? Megan got out of bed, curious in spite of herself, and opened the door a crack. More laughter. She crept down the stairs and stopped at the landing, listening around the corner.

Her father said, "It's starting to look like a turkey to me. What do you think?"

Jeremy hesitated. "Well, not exactly like a turkey. It needs legs. Hey, I know."

The refrigerator door opened. "How about these drumsticks? They're leftovers, but—"

"Great! We can just stick them in the potatoes."

Megan made her way slowly to the kitchen door and watched her father and Jeremy working over a strange brown mound. The floor creaked and they looked up.

"Come see!" her father said. "We've got ourselves a turkey after all."

Megan stepped into the kitchen and studied the shape. "What is it?" she asked.

"Let me tell," said Jeremy. "I helped think of it. First, try to guess what's under the mashed potatoes."

"Those are the potatoes? But why are they that color?"

"It's gravy—to make it look roasted like a turkey. But guess what's underneath."

"I can't imagine," Megan said.

"Meatloaf!" Jeremy answered, beaming. "Three of them. They're still frozen, but Dad sawed them in half and we put the stuffing in between. Pretty neat, huh? We just have to get the frosting—I mean the potatoes—smoothed out a little better."

Megan watched in amazement as her father stuck a drumstick on each side of the mound. Jeremy started to spread potatoes over them, then stopped. He handed the knife to Megan.

"Here, you try," he said.

Megan swirled the potatoes up and over the drumsticks carefully. She stepped back and looked at her work.

"This is great. How'd you ever think of it?"

Jeremy laughed. "Remember that volcano I made for the science fair last year out of papier-mâché? Well, this is like that. I call it potato-mâché."

CHAPTER

TWENTY

egan saw the station wagon pull into the driveway and ran ahead of her father and Jeremy to meet it. Her mother stepped out, looking tired, but her face lit up when she saw Megan.

She hugged Megan close, then held her at arm's length. "Look how you've grown! Is it possible? Or maybe I'm just used to smaller children. Oh, can you get Josh out of his car seat while I help Edith?"

The passenger door opened, and Edith, her back rigid, slowly set her feet on the ground.

A second car, carrying Uncle Joe and Andrew, pulled

into the drive. Hugs were exchanged all around, everyone making sure to hug everyone else, like clinking glasses when someone says a toast. And then they all started toward the house, all talking at once and bumping into each other.

Josh toddled along next to Megan, his little hand wrapped tightly around her finger.

"Mom, can I talk to you for a minute?" Megan called ahead.

Her mother was sandwiched between Mr. Alexander and Jeremy, one arm around each. Megan tried to hurry along. She had wanted to see her mother alone, to prepare her for the surprise, to break the news by herself.

"Mom!" she called again, but her mother had already disappeared into the house.

As Megan helped Josh up the steps, she heard her mother in the kitchen.

"What is that heavenly smell? And the oven is warm!"

Megan lifted Josh to her hip and carried him inside. Her mother had turned on the oven light and was leaning over, peeking in through the glass door.

"For goodness' sake!" she exclaimed. "What is that?"

Andrew stood next to her, looking, too. "Turkey," he said proudly.

Mr. Alexander smiled and winked at Megan.

"See—me see, too," Josh demanded in Megan's ear.

"Mom, can we talk now? Here Josh, go see cousin Jeremy."

Megan grabbed her mother's arm, pulled her into the living room, and sat her down in a chair.

Her mother leaned forward. "What is it, honey? What's going on?"

Megan had been rehearsing her speech in front of the bathroom mirror. But now, with her mother perched on the edge of the chair, her face puzzled and worried, Megan forgot what she had wanted to say. She could hear Jeremy's squeaky voice in the kitchen. "Meatloaf!" he was saying. There was a swell of laughter.

"Yes?" her mother said, gripping the arms of the chair. "Oh, look. Your grandparents just pulled in. I really must get back—"

This was harder than Megan had expected. The bathroom mirror had just sat there, letting her take her time.

She remembered the first part of her speech. "I wanted to surprise you and have Thanksgiving dinner here." She couldn't remember the next part. The back door was opening. She hurried on, just saying whatever popped into her head. "But everything went wrong—I couldn't get the potatoes home by myself, and then Bachmann's was all filled up—"

"But honey, I made reservations for us. Don't you remember?"

"I know, but I cancelled them, and then we—Jeremy and I—had to drag the turkey home in the snow. And it would have worked, too, except the raccoons or something took it off the porch. So we—Jeremy and Dad, really—had to use meatloaf, instead. That's what you saw in the oven—meatloaf, frosted with mashed potatoes."

Mrs. Alexander's face started to wrinkle up. Her bottom lip trembled.

Megan talked faster.

"I'm sorry," she said. "I really tried. But it wasn't my fault, at least not about the raccoons."

Mrs. Alexander blinked, releasing two big tears that rolled down her cheeks. Megan felt angry, helpless. She hated to see her mother cry, especially when she was the reason for it.

She patted her mother's back. "I'm sorry. It was supposed to be a nice surprise, but it just turned out all wrong. I'm really sorry. Don't cry, please."

Mrs. Alexander wiped at her eyes with the back of her hand. "Sorry?" she said. "Whatever for? This is the very nicest thing you've ever done for me!"

CHAPTER
TWENTY-ONE

"Ta-da" Mr. Alexander said, carefully setting the big platter at the head of the table. Everyone applauded.

Grandpa Alexander gave Megan's shoulder a little squeeze. "You've done a mighty fine job, young lady. Your grandmother and I are honored to be here."

"We all are," said Grandma Moore. "This is much nicer than a restaurant. Now that"—she pointed to the platter— "is what I call real home cooking."

Megan looked at the table with pride, at the steaming dishes of creamed onions and succotash, at the rolls nestled in a linen napkin.

Josh patted the tray on his high chair with his hands and sang out, "Tur—tur—key!"

Mr. Alexander laughed and made a great show of sharpening the carving knife, drawing the long blade back and forth against the sharpening stone. "I think we're all ready," he said. "Now, let us pray.

"Heavenly Father, we are gathered together today to give thanks for our many blessings. Usually we are in such a hurry to carve the turkey that maybe we don't listen to the blessing as carefully as we should. But today, our turkey is a little, uh, unusual, and perhaps we're not in such a hurry to eat."

Megan squirmed at the way her father said the blessing—not praying exactly but more like talking, so that it seemed rude not to pay attention. She wondered if God felt the same way. Mr. Alexander continued.

"We have had a long week, but a good one, and we have learned many things. Megan got us thinking about tradition, and she tried hard to prepare a traditional Thanksgiving meal for us all. She would have done it, too, if you had not decided that some of your little creatures deserved a special Thanksgiving meal of their own.

"But I have learned today that a traditional Thanksgiving is more than a turkey and all the trimmings. It is family, gathered together, giving thanks for each other, for the love we share throughout the year, for the blessings of plentiful food, for warmth and shelter."

Mr. Alexander paused and the room was silent. Megan jumped when she heard her mother's voice.

"Before you say 'Amen,' dear, I want to say something. Today I am especially thankful for my lovely family, for Megan's hard work and good intentions. But even more than that, I am grateful for the way she and Jeremy worked together to make this meal happen."

"I want to add something, too," Aunt Edith said. "I want to give thanks for my sister, who came when I needed help, who worked hard all week giving love and attention to my children instead of her own."

Aunt Edith stopped talking. Megan opened one eye and peeked around the table. Aunt Edith was dabbing her eyes with her napkin, but everyone's head was still bowed. It was hard to tell if this was still a prayer.

Grandpa Moore cleared his throat. "As long as this blessing is turning into a free-for-all, I would just like to say—and I'm sure I speak for all the old folks here—that I am very thankful for the two daughters we raised, for their wonderful husbands, and for our four handsome grandchildren—two of whom made this meal possible."

Grandpa Alexander broke in. "Indeed we are

thankful, especially for the way Megan brought us all together today under this roof."

There was another pause, and Megan felt she was supposed to say something. "Jeremy really helped— with his skateboard and the potatoes—and Dad, too. They made the turkey."

"Amen," said Mr. Alexander.

"Wait a minute," Jeremy said. "I didn't get a turn. I wanted to say that this is like the first Thanksgiving, the one my essay is about. The Pilgrims didn't always have turkey either—only if they could find it. They had to harvest their crops and hunt for food, maybe in the snow, maybe fighting off raccoons, or even wolves—"

"Wolves!" repeated Andrew, pulling at Aunt Edith's dress.

"I think that's enough, Jeremy," Mr. Alexander said. "You don't want to frighten the little ones. Well now, have you all had your say? Yes? Then, Amen."

"Amen," everyone repeated. Heads were lifted slowly.

Mr. Alexander rubbed his hands together. "Now, how do I carve this thing?"

The long knife cut though the mound of potatoes, through the meatloaf, through the stuffing. Mr. Alexander pulled out a long, thin slice, slid it onto a plate, and handed it down the table.

"Pass the rolls, please," Aunt Edith said, breaking one in half for Josh.

The food started around the table. Jeremy heaped a spoonful of succotash onto his plate. He looked closely at his big slice of meatloaf and smiled.

"Pass the ketchup," he said.

TWENTY-TWO

Megan sat at her desk, tapping her teeth with the end of a pencil. The house was quiet again except for the sound of her parents in the kitchen, washing the last of the dishes.

The back door slammed and Megan looked out the window. In the yellow square of light from the kitchen she could see Jeremy crossing the yard, a paper plate of leftovers sagging in his hands. The beam of a flashlight danced down the slope to the thicket. The light shone into the opening in the branches. Jeremy was just visible in the dim light as he knelt down and shoved the paper plate into the little clearing.

Megan raised her hand to knock on the window, then stopped. She watched him for a moment, smiling to herself, before she returned to work.

Megan got out her essay and found the two empty pages titled "The Turkey" and "The Blessing." She stared at them for a long time. Then she took all the pages she had written, gathered them together into a neat stack, and tore them in half.

She pulled out a fresh piece of paper and wrote across the top:

WHAT THANKSGIVING MEANS TO ME

She skipped two lines, indented, and started writing. And this time she didn't even stop to count the words.

Rainbow Bridge®

The Worst Christmas Ever
by Connie Remlinger-Trounstine
0-8167-3516-6 $2.95

No Boys Allowed
by Marilyn Levinson
0-8167-3136-5 $2.95
Coming in December 1994

And an exciting new series . . .

WELCOME INN
by E.L. Flood

Secret in the Moonlight
0-8167-3427-5 $2.95

Ghost of a Chance
0-8167-3428-3 $2.95

The Skeleton Key
0-8167-3429-1 $2.95
Coming in December 1994

The Spell of the Black Stone
0-8167-3579-4 $2.95
Coming in January 1995

Available wherever you buy books.